SOOTHING THOUGHTS

MOHAMMAD SOLTANIAN

ISBN 979-888629320-3

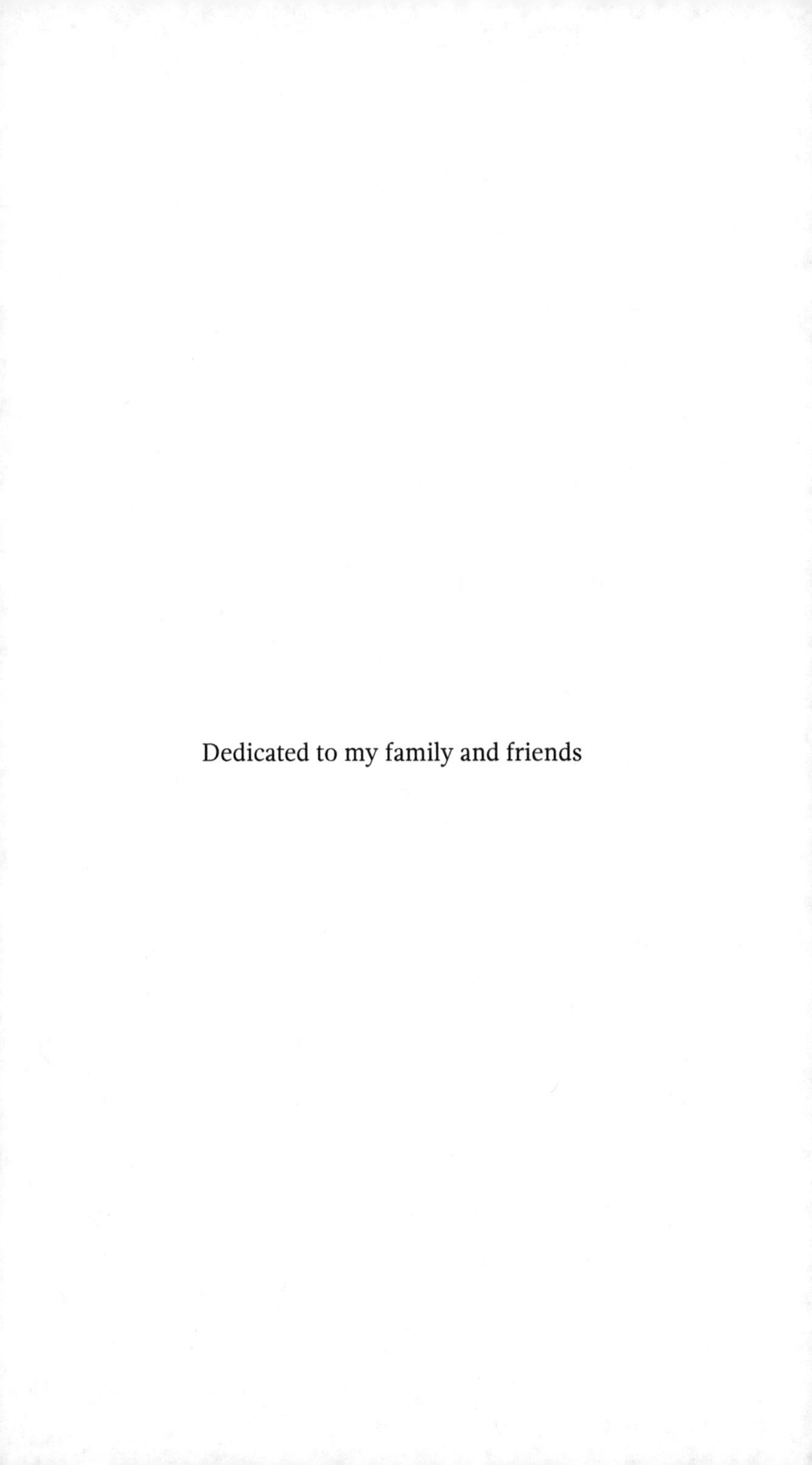

Dedicated to my family and friends

Contents

CHAPTER ONE

WHEN IT STARTED

Imagine yourself on your first trip after you graduate from university. I had few choices based-on my budget, so after searching a lot about a different country, I noticed that I had two easy options searching for a whole new world. Malaysia and Thailand were countries that had other stories from my own country Iran. After searching a lot and talking to many friends who experienced at least one of them, I decided to visit Malaysia as many of my friends had already visited Thailand and could describe it for me, so Malaysia was a new country for my close friends' circle. I had no idea how this trip was going to change my viewpoint for good. Seven hours from Tehran to Kuala Lumpur was an excellent opportunity for me to sleep and be fresh when I landed in KL.

When I received the KL and found a place to stay, I noticed that things were very different in my country. The most obvious difference was the driving system that cars move in an opposite direction with Iran. Searching about colonial time in Malaysia and finding places to eat was all I could do on my first day. Renting a condominium helped me to be in a delightful atmosphere that flowed in my neighborhood. When I went to my bed, I started thinking that this trip took only seven hours for me, but one or two hundred years ago, this trip could have a different story!!

I thought at the same time with me; there are many tourists from other countries that we could meet. Thanks to the internet era, we can search on the internet and find new friends from different countries and cultures. It is something that our predecessors couldn't even dream it. We can fall in love and marry each other and live in another country! Until the following day, these thoughts were with me that I decided to give it a chance and try to find the love of my life or at least a lifetime girlfriend in KL.

Early morning, I woke up and got ready to explore the city, especially the most iconic place where I could probably find a girlfriend; for sure, my choice was the KLCC area and, more specifically, inside the twin towers.

The central court, as I expected, was full of locals and tourists that created a positive atmosphere for everyone. Chinese, Indians, Australians, European tourists, and other nations made my plan look easy!

Bon chance!! A very calm song could be heard in the court. So how should I start, and what are my standards?

My dear readers, if you think it is a familiar story with some predictable ups and downs or exaggerations, you are wrong!!

I will not even try to create a Proustian moment for you, so stay relaxed and go on.!!!

The first idea was finding my soulmate by sorting nations alphabetically, Australians, Chinese, Indians, etc.

It looked too racist even to me, so I decided to respect locals and start dating Malay girls to find my true love.

But how should I find someone serious? Yes, the internet can help me to find and set a date with a girl.

After searching for a couple of hours in different apps and websites, I found a girl that was close to my standards.

After texting for hours when she heard my idea about the marriage with someone from another culture and only when she got sure that I was serious, we were sitting face to face in the Starbucks branch on the 3rd floor of the twin towers. She was a cute girl wearing a hijab as she was in her photos. We were both surprised because her English accent wasn't clear for me and later I noticed that I was too hairy in her eyes!!

She liked my initial idea, and we started to know each other. Suddenly I remembered that she didn't use her real name on the website and asked her name. Nur! She replied politely, and I said that I used my real name, which is Mohammad. I explained that besides her, I plan to date many other girls while I am in her hometown, and she agreed to be open in our relationship as long as it is accepted in her culture. The coffee was good, and we enjoyed walking and shopping in twin towers for 3-4 hours as talking about our plans and hopes. Everything went on very well, and I decided to buy her a gift to remember that particular date. She refused politely, and we said goodbye. We agreed to think about ourselves and be in touch.

Now that Nur is gone, I am still in the towers and searching for something to eat because I cannot be okay with Malay food, so I am limited to fast food until I find a good restaurant. A Fuel Shack branch was the most attractive option as we do not have its branch in Iran.

I ordered an original shack and started to review my day and dialogues with Nur.

Oh my God, what should I do for breakfast? I can't cook, and I have nothing in my condominium.

I took a taxi and left the towers. Later at night, I wanted to continue chatting with Nur, but I thought it could mean bad in the Islamic culture, so I kept searching for new Malay cases.

The next day, when I wanted to visit new places in the KL, I saw Sofia. A Malay girl with a better English accent guided me to find some addresses. She also told me that if I am looking for girls, I should visit Bukit Bintang in the evening, in which I have a better chance to find new girls. When I explained my goal from dates, she liked it, and we exchanged our numbers to make a date later in the evening.

Sofia was a great girl with self-confidence, high heels, and a great taste in fashion. The way that she appeared as the opposite of Nur. As a Muslim, I tried to ignore this difference and accept all kinds of cultures and mindsets that I could face in this or upcoming dates. To be honest with my readers, I should say during my dates. There were moments that I was searching back in my mind that if there was any way to kiss those girls with no sin? And my date with Sofia included many moments like this!! I never wanted to drink or smoke, she understood it, and we shared our story of life.

When I asked directly about her marriage viewpoint, she gazed down and told me about her family and her desire to stay in KL for the rest of her life as she enjoyed her healthy lifestyle and middle-class family. To describe her, I can say she was a brown hair girl with cute eyes and an Asian mindset to love and marriage based on her concentrate on her current and possible future family. As we walked in the Bukit Bintang, she showed me some shopping malls and local markets that were good places to find clothes and used computers. We went to a McDonald's branch near the monorail station, which was surprisingly crowded at that time. She taught me some new Malay words, such as Selamat dating, Harga, Jalan, etc. I told her that I usually play in chess tournaments during my leisure time, and she showed me some tennis videos on her phone that could explain why her body was that in shape. Talking with Sofia and hearing her memories since her childhood made me think that she is not just a cute girl, and I can go deeper into her character. We both were talkative and tried to know each other more and more. Sofia had already visited some European and African countries, and her knowledge of western literature had impressed me. We got more serious, and I asked about her views about my plan, and I asked if she had the same fantasy. Like many other people worldwide, she already thought about this idea and mentioned that she prefers to see many people and create her international friends' circle, but marriage has a different story in her view of life. Later we exchanged our favorite songs, and she texted me that she participated in Metallica's concert held a couple of years ago in the Merdeka stadium that wasn't close to the city center.

It was getting late, so we agreed to share a taxi for our destinations. We said goodbye, and we promised to ponder our date and our philosophy of life and set another date until I am in KL.

Although using online platforms could provide you with an ocean of possibilities, there were funny moments in my searches that made me laugh after these years. Different profile photos with the actual person happened in many cases that made me ask for video calls before my following dates with many girls.

To make it clear for my readers, it should be mentioned it wasn't an easy process for me to find a place to date another tourist in the KL. In most cases, they were in a hurry and wanted to visit places that I already did or vice versa.

As a Muslim, I never wanted to date in pubs, so I had to find a perfect place to meet tourists. I searched on the internet for new girls for a couple of days while I got used to taking long-hour walks in the city to explore new places. What makes KL an extraordinary place as a middle eastern guy is its rainy days that we could rarely experience on that scale. For the first days of my trip to Malaysia, I limited myself to KFC, McDonald's, and Fuel Shack, so it was a great experience to find some Iranian restaurants near Bukit Bintang. New places for meals gave me the self-confidence to visit more places that were far from the KLCC area, but still, where ever I was, I preferred to back to the Petronas twin towers for its spectacular view during sunset. It was where I could meet more tourists in the Kinokuniya book shop. After talking about my idea to many other tourists in the book shop, most of them refused to set a date with me as they thought it would be a very shallow relationship by its nature, and it was never going to end well.

In some cases, what I experienced was a perfect example of orientalism-related thoughts and misunderstandings that could be mentioned in a whole different story. They were times that I just wanted to call Nur or Sofia for our second date, but I never wanted to seem like a guy that lost his motivation, so I didn't resign. In short stories or even novels, it takes 2-3 paragraphs for readers when the writer finds new characters, but it looks like an endless and sometimes meaningless process in the real world. After visiting Batu caves and some Chinese temples, I met an Australian family and asked that family's father about my marriage idea. It seemed that he had thought about this fantasy when he was younger, so he had no problem that I shared my opinion with his beautiful daughter. It was funny that the whole family participated in our subject as we were talking. If someone is serious, there is no fear to see the family of the other side of the relation, and visiting the whole family at once and getting close to all of them without having initial privacies were too funny and odd. We all noticed and laughed about it, and surprisingly we all were okay to sit there and let our imagination go further many things. I exchanged numbers with all of them, and we separated with the hope of seeing that fantastic family very soon. I am a Gemini! The first words Mia told me on our first semi-private date as all her family came to shop with her and were close to us in the Starbucks. It was a surprise because I am a June Gemini too, but I don't believe many things that people say about my sign. What are your hobbies? she asked politely, and I explained to her how much I like participating in chess tournaments and reading books and outdoor activities.

We kept talking about our plans and things we like to do soon. Mia had a very cheerful lifestyle, and her view of life impressed me a lot. Part of her mindset, I think, came from an affluent family that she had and never had to be worried about basic things in her life. We ordered our second coffees, and for the rest of the date, we laughed at some jokes that we remembered from our own cultures. Mia was the first girl that I met for the second time in KL. We decided to take a long walk in the city instead of going to pubs or any other place. We wanted to enjoy nature inside the city. When I saw her near Jalan Raja Chulan on our second date, she was wearing her blue Nike shoes and white pants and a light blue T-shirt. She was like an angel, and it was one of the other moments that I wanted to forget my whole religious belief system!!!

She started making fun of me for being that hairy, and we spent a couple of hours in the streets of Kuala Lumpur before getting hungry and having to find food. When we were in China Town, she bought many gifts for her close friends and started sharing our photos to see how they felt about me in their group!! I should mention that their responses were too funny to be reflected here.

I understood that you don't just link to a person or a family in marriage. You will find a new society and culture that should be understood or tolerated for the rest of your life that was too scary for me. I always believed that visiting other countries with a wife is disappointing because as soon as she gets pregnant, you cannot feel the same adventures with each other, and I told that to Mia. I was waiting for a plea from her side to say that this was not true, but she admitted that scenario that scared me even more. It was one of the moments that I wanted to forget her and all other girls' beauty and forget about the whole marriage thing. We were talking about a normal lifestyle in our future when we found a KFC branch. While I was in KL, I discovered that I couldn't order KFC without cheesy wedges, and I should emphasize that it must be tested by all tourists as long as they are in Malaysia. After talking and walking a lot, we joined her family in the Star bucks, and we got sure that we would continue our friendship for a lifetime. It was time to say goodbye, and I had no idea how I ganna live without her. I saw three girls in this city, and all I found was happiness and positive energy. I knew that we would text each other for weeks or months daily, but our feelings may wane after a while, and I could feel empty again.

For me, back to everyday life takes time, and sometimes it gets a lot of energy and attention from me. I had a feeling to stop searching and pick one of them as my soulmate, but at first, I had to be sure about their feelings too, so I decided to call Nur again.

When I called Nur, we both had a couple of days to ponder more about our shared fantasy. I thought that there was a mutual feeling among us that said it was too soon to talk about the next steps, and on the other hand, we had not that much time to know each other better. I was about to back to my own country, and she got more involved in her job. For me, lack of time in this part of my trip meant an unwanted goodbye to three fabulous girls and a magnificent country with fantastic nature and very welcome people. As I was getting ready to reach my flight, I thought love is a sweet thing even if you cannot find your soulmate on your first attempt. I knew that still, I had a chance with three of them, but what if my foreign lover is neither Malay nor Australian? Does it mean maybe I should stay in Iran and wait for tourists that will visit my hometown? Who knows? Perhaps I need to search in other places around the world. Saying goodbye in this situation is hard for me, but among all of us, Mia reacted more relaxed that maybe it was because of her culture or financial status that made her able to visit many more countries, and she was affluent enough to visit my country if she wanted. Sofia wanted to visit Turkey in her upcoming holidays that could be extended enough to come to Iran too. Having special moments with all of them never concluded that which one is the love of my life. Maybe I should feel extraordinary moments when I am looking at their eyes or body; after all, I am not the type of guy who would get too excited, so I tried to postpone my final verdict to another time that we have a better mutual understanding. Thanks to the internet, it could happen nowadays, something that our predecessors couldn't even dream it. It seems that in an old-fashion cliché, I can finish every chapter of this book with this phrase, but in the following chapters, you will see that I plan to ponder on issues that readers in the future get surprised by the depth of thoughts in our generation. Is it possible? It's for the next generation of readers to judge!

CHAPTER TWO

After coming back to my country, I faced many questions by myself. How many countries should I visit before my final decision? How many girls should I meet? How should I pick one of my three friends in Malaysia? Is it rational to be limited to foreigners? I had thousands of this type of questions, and being far from my friends had impacted my performance in daily challenges. After searching many different books and motivation courses, I concluded that I don't want to listen to any of them, and I want to have my system. I promised myself to ask and give only one chance to each person because I noticed that there are surely more than one million girls around my age in the world that I have not enough time in my life to say Hello to all of them. I had to decide between three good girls that I had no idea about their past and had no challenges. All people are good or could be tolerated in the short-term, but when talking about a lifetime issue, things ganna change rapidly. After my trip, the first video call was about this issue and how each one of them could think about the difference between short-term and long-term relations. Nur once told me that she is still a great fan of my idea but, as a religious girl, cannot put more time and energy into this lifestyle and wants to get married soon instead of waiting for someone from abroad. We agreed to be lifetime friends and closed our marriage scenario.

It is a good feeling when you find such a lifetime friend that you are sure that it is approximately impossible to forget her or see her again face to face. I already knew that I was not the only guy in my two other friends' lives, so I had to be fast and honest with them too. I knew that Nur as a Muslim is more close to my belief system, and Mia has the closest personality to me, so I thought Sofia is someone in between that could be a better option to get involved in the long-term because of the way that I looked to Mia was too exciting, and I needed a slower pace in my relationship with her.

Is it normal that I decide for my whole life based on some stereotypes created by others? Who said that it is better to avoid excitement in life? If my friends can be happy in my absence, I can be happy too, so I told myself: let's go on!!!

I should find where are the most beautiful girls in the world. After searching too many websites, I liked some photos that belonged to South American girls from brazil and Uruguay. I also found Kenyan and swiss girls very attractive, but the most obvious choices were eastern European girls that were close to my country. Where should I go to visit them? It was one of the many times that stereotypes influenced me. I promised myself to visit Armenia, the first Christian country in the world, to find my soulmate. Later I will explain why at that time it was a mistake!!.

Back to the three girls that I followed in every possible platform, I saw Mia's photos in bikini style in her hometown that showed me how easy it could be for someone in his/her life. I liked that life never stopped for her, and she is going on in her life waiting for me and open to any new options. Sofia also continued to be the kind of girl that brings happiness to every room that they are.

As a June Gemini, I prefer cheerful and crowded places where positive energy can be felt in the atmosphere. When I visited Yerevan, it was many last seconds offer for Istanbul in Iran that my friends later told me that it was a high season tourist month in Turkey, and I lost an opportunity to visit Turkey with those promotions in flight prices.

When I received the house that I already shared with some other friends of mine, I noticed we would have language issues during our trip as Armenians do not speak English fluently in most parts of Yerevan, and my Russian was not that fluent to effectively communicating with them.

At the time that I visited Yerevan, I preferred to walk in the city and tried to cover my needed things near the most iconic place that was republic square or, as Armenians used to say, Hraparak.

If you are looking for an old-fashion theme in everything and you want to stay away from your world for 2-3 days, and you plan to smoke and drink as much as your body allows, Yerevan could be an adventure for you. As a tourist looking for very crowded places, it wasn't a good choice, but I never want to deny the fact that it backs to my character, not my trip destination and great Armenian people. Arpine, a girl that I met in a restaurant, promised to show me some churches and places that could be interesting. I wanted to talk to her about my marriage theory, but I thought it is too soon and would be odd to start my first line with my idea, so I kept it for myself as Armenians are very rigid in the case of marriage with a Muslim back to their historical tensions with their neighbors. Fortunately, Arpine was a smart girl that never started smoking like many other people around her age. She showed me a very famous supermarket that could be found here and there in the city called SAS as I remember. The positive point about Armenian girls is that although they are not Muslims, they understand Islamic culture as many of them have family members in Iran, and they are familiar with our culture. I was lucky enough to find a Russian girl that was a business owner in a church, and it was the time that I grabbed my chance and invited her to join Arpine and me for a meal. She agreed to join us, but it was clear that she was joining us mostly because of her curiosity rather than anything else; later, she explained she got bored during her trip and wanted to find random friends that were okay by me. When we sat at our table, Nadia told us that she planned to open a new disco in Yerevan and she was excited about that. Two girls got busy with the business plan, and I was trying to read the Armenian alphabet on the menu, trying to find halal food for myself. They wanted to have a drink with their food, and as a Muslim, I was not allowed to pay for alcoholic drinks based on my religious thoughts. I explained the situation to them, and they found it odd because their food was more expensive than a drink. I explained the religious issue, and they politely agreed to pay for their drink. Now that we talked about culture and religion, it was the best time to share my idea with them. Both of them laughed and said it was too shallow, and they were not interested in that scenario as they prefer a real relationship with someone from their own culture. They both told me that instead of this crazy idea, I need to pay for sex in my trips and not get involved with just a person. Seeing other girls and tourists in Yerevan, most of them had the same opinion and encouraged me to change my life view. In some cases, their invitation to a new lifestyle was combined to encourage me to change my religion. I was okay with my religion and refuted their idea politely.

Dear readers, for those of you with a reading habit, I should say if my trip to Yerevan were a book, for sure the writer was Heinrich Boll, and I felt the atmosphere of his books in my daily life in this city. I was the clown with a different view than the society around him with his logic and belief system. What made me close to Boll's clown was that I was losing money in a city that was not suitable for me. I decided to return to Iran very soon and save my money for my next trip, so I got sure that I would receive the next flight in 48 hours. I knew that my plan wouldn't work in this city, so I tried enjoying the adventure in this country and concentrated on foods, halal drinks, and of course, spectacular views.

Natakhtari, a Georgian non-alcoholic drink, was the most memorable thing that I found in Yerevan. Later I asked Arpine about a song that could be heard in most restaurants of the city called Yerevan Erebuni. All I can remember is two names in that song, Masis, and Arax, as symbols of the town!!

Spending some time in Yerevan mall and local markets made me think more about Armenian culture and language and how economic challenges had affected the lifestyle of the youth in this country.

Buying some souvenirs from local shops that had the Armenian alphabet on them makes me remember the days that I had in Yerevan. Being in an Iranian concert on the final day of my trip and making some Iranian friends reminds me of the feeling that I had. I saw how shallow is my thoughts for people that don't know me. I saw no one try to live in my fantasy world for even a couple of hours or at least from the start till the end of a meal. Maybe it was necessary for me to get this lesson that no one cares about me outside my family and close friend circle. I just wanted to listen to something during my flight to Tehran, and I had no problem listening to it over and over. It was not hard for me to find a perfect song for my mood at that time, Ode to my family by cranberries, splendid dear Dolores, splendid indeed.

Although my trip to Armenia could be considered as a fiasco based on my purpose, it made me stick to my family and hometown for a while, where I could enjoy the beauty of Isfahan and familiar people in my life. I told Sofia about my trip, and she explained that her plan to visit turkey had changed, and she plans to visit Iran before visiting Turkey with her Japanese friend. Sofia told me that she would come to Iran two months later, and they wanted to visit Isfahan. It was because she started searching about Iran after our first date and liked historical places such as Naghshe Jahan square or Vank cathedral in my hometown. I asked about her friend, and she mentioned that she is a girl about our age and her name is Yukari. She explained that, unlike what I think, Yukari is a Christian, and she has already visited many places, including Turkey that made her eager to visit Iran before visiting Turkey for the second time. Sofia also told me that she mentioned that she shared my idea about marriage, and Yukari liked it. I had no idea that if I was allowed to ask Sofia to let me date her friend, I tried to postpone it till the time that didn't scare any of them. I never wanted to look the bad guy in her eyes, and I still had no idea how Yukari looked, so being patient was the best solution until we joined each other.

I was glad that I left Armenia sooner than I planned because I saved some money, and the fact that my friends will join me in two months gave me enough energy to stick to my work and save my money to make my next trip in a nearer future.

I was being depressed from what I experienced on the one hand and the fact that my relationship with my eastern friends was better than what I expected after several months provided a unique situation in my life till that time. What if other people in the world think and react like what girls did on my last trip?

This experience made me limit myself for a while to apps that could translate my chat simultaneously to the language of my friend on the other side of the call. This is a new phenomenon that helped me to stay optimistic about my future search in countries that I have no idea about their languages. I learned a new lesson in my internet-based searches. When we are talking about unlimited possibilities, there is no majority in it. I mean, in a situation that I know, many random guys on the internet are boys pretending to be girls. Still, I cannot conclude that all my fake friends were boys or robots. For sure, sometimes I stuck with the wrong girls that wanted to make money from their friendship with me. There were time periods that I used to chat with more than five girls, and after they noticed that they could not make money from me, they started showing their private area to show me that they were boys and made fun of me for the time that we had online chats. I am sure that happened for a vast majority of people around the world. Although it is bothering most of us, we have to admit that it is a new phenomenon that the internet gave us, and our predecessors couldn't even dream of it. Now that I am looking back, I can see that I am happy that we are in an era where people have more opportunities to show their real personalities. It used to bother me that people that I like cheated on me or left me alone, and now that I remember my life, I can guarantee that I never had regret to enjoying my life believing them and being part of their games. These all are small moments that could help our brain to be more effective in the future. I thought no one could be trusted or understood or even be ignored as we all have possibilities to surprise each other. The fact that even that mindset couldn't last that long with me gave me this ability to avoid judging people and let the time show me their real personalities. Maybe I had a trust issue at that time because all of a sudden, I found myself in chats that belonged to a ten-day period, and I stocked with new friends in Malaysia again. I thought it is not normal when you want to have a worldwide view and experience back to your safe zone and try to hide from challenges. It was thoughts that made me search other places in the world before my guests came to my hometown. Once I was playing in an online chess tournament. I tried to ask people about the country or city that they wished to visit once in their life. I am sure that if I keep doing that for many years, it is just a small possibility to face this answer in a minor majority of the society that I picked. You can't believe that most players told me, Kenya!! While I was waiting for a very rich or very crowded country. It was the only reason that I started searching for friends in this country. At first, I asked people in chess chatrooms, and later that I searched the country and culture, I started chatting with some random girls. Nairobi is a place with welcome people who will guide you clearly when you ask them about what you need as a tourist. While I was living in my fantasy world, I noticed that I needed some real people around me. Once I noticed that I changed my sleep pattern just for being online, to chat with people who are awake and not do the same thing for me. I am sure that many people have that kind of lifestyle that cyberspace has become their real-world in recent years. For a while, many of us had more online friends and activities than in real life. We even working inline nowadays and our income depends on this lifestyle and pace of life. Once a guy explained to me that the most famous girls in Kenya for their beauty are from a tribe called Kamba. For me, that beauty was getting a more important factor. It was a forward step to search for girls in a country that I had never been to based on their tribes. I personally searched among many tribes such as Luhya, Kamba, Kikuyu, Luo, Kisii, and Kamba to see what type of cultural information I needed before visiting that country. I met many wonderful girls with great personalities in Nairobi while searching from home, and we became lifetime friends before I even went there. They taught me the word Mpenzi which means darling in Swahili, and told me many things about their culture, places, and foods.

Getting involved with new friends in Kenya, I remembered that Sofia and Yukari would come to Isfahan in a week. It was odd that while I was learning about a new culture, a friend from another culture that was a newcomer to my life was about to visit.

I asked many friends in Isfahan and double-checked with Sofia the places that they preferred to visit or places that they had no idea about them but as tourists, they need to visit.

CHAPTER THREE

Finally, they arrived at Isfahan and went to a hotel in the city center area as they told me they were not ready to come to my place on the first day. We talked on the phone, and they told me that they wanted to visit Naghshe Jahan square and local shops at first. I told them that I would pick them up in front of their hotel the next morning. I asked them to be prepared for a long walk, and they agreed.

I think it is a problem for all Muslims around the world how to say hello to a non-Muslim girl in a polite way as we do not shake hands with girls, and sometimes we want to understand other religions and do not want to be rigid about ours. Fortunately, Sofia had told Yukari the way that we behave, and both of them were very understanding and ready for cultural shocks that they would face in their trip to Iran. We walked from their hotel to the Naghshe Jahan square, and they told me about their trip to Iran and the first impression of our country on them. I found Yukari a genius that already knew many things about my country and culture. She already had an impressive knowledge about historical places in Isfahan and talked about the aspect of culture that is interesting for her about Iran. We took a lot of photos, and it was only after lunch that we found enough time to talk about my marriage idea. She told us that the Japanese are hard workers, and sometimes it looks like a good idea in her mind that marry a foreigner and live in a country with a slower pace of life. I saw that it looks like Sofia doesn't feel bad when we talk, and her friend is involved with the marriage idea. All men know that it would be a sign that Sofia was not that serious in our relationship, and her behavior was telling me that. They told me that they had busy days before their flight and still they are jetlagged, so they asked me to have a short meeting for that day as they wanted to sleep very soon. We created a Whatsapp group, and I turned them to their hotel. I told them that I would pick them up and they should come to my place to visit my family and be our guest for lunch the next day. They agreed as they already knew that it would be a cultural event in my country!!

Tomorrow morning, when I picked them up in front of their hotel, both of them had worn a hijab as they wanted to respect our culture, which was very important for both of them. I explained to them that we had time, and it was better to visit some local markets before going to our home. It looked that they had enough sleep as both of them were very energetic and participated in a long talk about marriage and their opinions about different levels of feelings when they are in love with someone. We talked about cultural issues and stereotypes worldwide, and It was a great surprise when I noticed that Yukari already knows Edward Said and watched his videos related to orientalism. Being with people like Yukari and Sofia goes in a way that you would forget about time and sexual issues. They showed that both of them had read many subjects during their life and can better off people around themselves mentally.

They bought many things from local markets, especially small carpets that made them stay and visit a local shop for more than 30 minutes.

It was a perfect time to show them how my friends circle spend time when we gather together. I called some friends of mine to meet each other in the evening

When we got home, I introduced them to my family, and they surprised us with two small gifts from Japan and Malaysia.

They liked Kebab and told us that they would remember their trip with our delicious food. Everything went on very friendly, and we kept sharing our future plans and our view on marriage. Yukari showed all of us how to use chopsticks that in Japanese called Hashi.

My parents couldn't speak English well enough to make a clear conversation with them, but I saw my Mom was looking at them as serious options for her son!! My Mom told me that she liked their behavior and wanted to see them again, and I should be serious with them about love. With that trend of love searching on the internet, I couldn't pick only one of them. Sofia, Mia, and now Yukari came into my life, and I wanted all of them. I am sure most of my readers had the same feelings when they were young. Sometimes I think most of us pretend that we are concentrated on just one girl. At least at that time, it was impossible for me to love just one person, and maybe it wasn't true love, but for me, it was an axiom that I wanted them all, and this pleasant fact already motivated me to search more and more girls before getting mingle.

Having some mature conversation, I wanted to create an extraordinary memory for my guests from Iran. I already knew about nature in Malaysia, and I google-searched about Yukari's hometown in Japan, A safari tour was the best gift for them as I thought it might be a different experience for them because of the difference between nature in our countries. Visiting a new aspect of nature for me in KL was terrific, and I thought it might have the same effect on them. My friends got everything ready for staying one night in a desert. Both Sofia and Yukari told me that it is the first time in their life that they could see the sky that clear, and they couldn't believe that the stars that they couldn't see in their everyday routine life were that beautiful. After gathering together near a fire and eating some different Iranian food that my friends brought, we started dancing and teaching my guests how fun our dance is in Iran and all over the middle east as some of my friends were originally Arab. Fortunately, they liked it and told us that they would keep watching that dances on the internet and practice them for the rest of their lives. My friends also liked Sofia and Yukari and tried to teach them some funny words and cultural behaviors that could only be seen in Iran. We slept that night in the Sahara, and although it was a bit cold, we slept very well, and no one got sick or tired the day after that. The girls in our group had started telling good things and funny memories about me to my guests and tried to help me in my relations. It was such a surprise even for me that on our way back, my friends invited Yukari and Sofia to a saloon to get their hair and nails done in a traditional Iranian way. They both acted like children and accepted the invitation. When we finally received in front of their hotel, they appreciated it and told us that they wanted to rest and would call me after one or two days. Weeks Later, Yukari messaged me and mentioned it was her first camping without alcoholic drinks, and she thought it was a new experience that never decreased the fun part of the camping for her.

Again I found myself in a positive atmosphere that gave me the courage to think about marriage because I already knew that this happy circle would disappear very soon, and I would be all by myself. The situation could be very depressing, but I knew it was necessary for achieving a better version of myself. When Sofia texted me in our Whatsapp group, I already knew that it was going to be our last meeting in Iran because they had to go to Turkey as they had already planned it.

Recently, I read a book called the philosopher and the wolf by Mark Rowlands. He mentioned two animals in his book (Wolf & Monkey) to describe people in the challenges of their life.

After reading that book, I asked myself why people should abuse each other to gain what they want, like monkeys, or why we should see ourselves in a competition or battlefield like Wolves?

I thought, why do we need to think about the life that harshly? For me, it was a meaningless view of life. I was so happy to see my friend's lifestyle that showed me other people around the world are looking at things like me. They wanted to enjoy their life not by abusing anyone, and it was a great moment in my life when they both told me that they think we are great friends, but neither of them can't decide about their marriage in a short trip. We all felt that we had our last chance to be that free and happy around each other, so we decided to make a great memory by sharing many photos on Instagram and visiting here and there in the city. I tried to feed them with all the delicious foods and drinks in Isfahan, and we bought souvenirs for each other. I bought a cross from an Armenian shop near the Vank cathedral in Isfahan for Yukari and a necklace for Sofia. Sofia, that already knew how much I admired her country, gave me a small size sculpture of twin towers, and Yukari gave me a bag that she told me using them is a trend among the youth in Japan at that time. We all agreed to think about each other and be in touch while we are open to new people in our lives. When we received in front of their hotel, Sofia bowed and sent a kiss from a distance to make fun of our limitations as Muslims, but Yukari had no idea about it, though she could not shake my hand probably I could hug her, so she gave me a big and long hug!! When we explained to her that it wasn't allowed in our culture, we all laughed a lot, and she apologized for that. We said goodbye in the big hope of seeing each other again even if I married neither of them!!!

When I found myself alone and empty two days after they left Iran, I backed to the searching habit. For me, it became such a routine that it reminded me of the running pattern of Murakami. I was running from this to that city around the world, learning some basic and nice words about their languages in the hope of finding the most attractive girl for myself. Although I was young, I never wanted to be the storyteller of Marcel Proust in my 50s. I never could see myself having a mantra to be calm. What I wanted was searching happiness in my way, albeit to me, sometimes it looked like mixing the methods that I read in books or ideas that I listen to music that I like. Searching on the internet was a way that I started, and it was getting lame to me. Imagine yourself randomly talking to people about your dreams while you are experienced enough to know the vast majority of them are not native English speakers, and many of them would not even try to translate some words that they don't know in your messages.

As most of the time in the year, chess platforms were full of great players from around the world, and I kept myself busy with chess tournaments and some piano lessons that could make me calm. Something had changed in my mind since Yukari hugged me. I am sure for her, it wasn't a way to express her lust in front of me and what I was feeling wasn't lust. She talked to me in that way. It was an appreciation. It was something that couldn't be said by words, and I was sure about that. I also was sure that she was right when she was telling me that she was not in that deep love with me. In my opinion, it was felt between two human beings regardless of their differences. When Yukari wanted to teach me how to work with the Japanese Hashi, she really wanted another guy to use something from her culture. She never wanted to culturally attack me, or telling me what is better or want is prohibited in her culture. What we shared wasn't that important in each other's lives to be claimed a dramatic change in our mindsets, but the way that we interacted gave both of us a new way of life.

After a couple of days, as we kept sharing our photos in our Whatsapp group, I remembered my promise to myself to go on to search for my new worlds. I told myself that I didn't want to have or make a stereotype about any nation, so I told myself that I should find an Eastern European girl. For me, it was better if she had some chess skills and could be a great rival in my chess tournaments.

My friend-making process in Nairobi was in a good situation, and every day I could find new gorgeous girls with positive mindsets about my idea about marriage, but which country in Europe should I search? I asked myself for a while. I decided that my international chess friends could guide me better than any other sources in cyberspace. After asking many friends of mine, they told me that Serbia has stunning and kind girls. As my friend claimed, they are mostly religious, and they can be a better experience for me as my friends told me about their experiences in chess tournaments. I started asking people in chess chatrooms with Serbian flags in front of their names if they were girls.

It was a funny moment most of the time as I wanted to do my searching process in the most random possible way.

Once, someone told me that she is a girl and asked me why I was looking for girls in Serbia? I replied politely and explained my intention, but I was ready to see a guy in my video call back in my mind. After two days of rejecting my video calls, she mentioned that she was a he and wanted to make fun of me. He told me that he liked my idea and wanted to help me instead of what he had done and wasted my time. I explained that I was ready for that because of my experiences in the past. He told me he likes that I am that crazy to keep my way with that system. My name is Vladimir, he said, and I introduced myself. Vladimir told me about his hometown called Novi Sad and told me that his hometown is the right place to find serious girls. After that, we became chess friends, and we had many matches daily when either of us had to get ready for a serious tournament. After a while that we got closer, he told me that he has a colleague that is older than me, but he thinks we are good guys, and he can introduce us together. Maja is her name, Vladimir said. Apparently, he told her about me a couple of days ago, and she liked my idea. Both of us agreed to exchange numbers through Vladimir. Again I should mention the ability that online chats gave me because Maja couldn't speak English fluently, and we had to use Serbian to English online dictionary in order to communicate with each other. Maja was a blonde and tall girl with a hardworking spirit. All of her family members were naturally strong, and she looked powerful too. Wooooowww, Yesss, Thank you, Vladimir, were the first words that I said in my mind when I had the first video chat with her. She noticed that I liked her style and laughed at me and said, you are not a good hider with her Serbian accent and body language. We introduced ourselves briefly, and I noticed that she likes to visit countries outside Europe, unlike most of her friends. She told me about her favorite chess champion, Alexander Alekhine, and the way that he played chess at that time. I think most players in the world would show great respect to Alekhine for what he has done for chess, and the fact that he is the only world chess champion that died while still was carrying his title makes him one of the greatest and smartest players of all time. After analyzing some of her games in her last tournament, she asked about my favorite champion, and I said Tigran Petrosian, the player that could be considered in a whole different world than Alekhine. We laughed at the difference between our views, and she searched some of my recent matches on the internet.

Being in touch with positive people brought happiness to my life, and I almost forgot about my fiasco on my trip to Yerevan. Maja was a very serious girl, and failure had no meaning for her. She told me that she works on herself to get better in all aspects of her life. She mentioned that she practices Muay Thai besides chess and hopes to be a good fighter in the near future. During my online and face-to-face meetings with girls, I never wanted to compare them with each other, but Maja's mindset was less girlish compared to all girls that I met till that time. To make it clear for my dear readers, just imagine a very hot girl that is ready to fight in the ring and is not damaged yet!! I mean a pure combination of being stylish and harsh. I never was more sure about any other girls in my dates than about Maja. Very quickly, I noticed that she is not mine! She never gave me the feeling that other girls gave me by picturing their future. Maja, even nowadays, is still a great chess friend, and with Vladimir, we analyze our games in chatrooms. As I noticed about Maja, love had different meanings for us, so we couldn't get involved in that way with each other.

While getting more involved with Maja, I noticed that one of my friends in Nairobi, whose name was Mueni, is working for a charity and helping other people, especially single moms.

Getting more involved with Kenyan friends, I noticed they have a great heart for sharing what they have with people they need. Compared to many nations, you could see people couldn't be considered a wealthy society but were strong enough to tolerate all challenges with each other. Mueni herself was a single mom that was lucky enough to find a job and cover her expenses successfully. She mentioned how she finally could start her business, and nowadays, she is hiring young single moms that have financial problems. Being in touch with Mueni showed me a new level of love for humanity. We talked a lot about different daily challenges for those ladies in their routine life. All I could do for her charity was use my chess society around the world to help those ladies. Mueni was that kind of friend that is always online, and you could depend on her when needed. We shared many photos and explained our goals and hopes in our life. She was the type of girl that had a hard life but finally could find her way to make money and protect her family. Once, she told me that even I could go on fewer trips and help people that really are on hard days. She explained that I didn't need to trust her and I could help my people in my hometown. What she used to say about helping other people was entirely right, and I promised myself to help people once I got a stable status. I noticed that she plans to put her life on this issue and probably has no time for another marriage in the near future. Whether she is a better person than me is for God to judge, but I had a dream, and I wanted to follow it till the day that my soulmate peacefully came to me. We agreed to continue our friendship and help each other when possible.

In my viewpoint, Kamba and Luo girls became the sexiest ladies in Kenya. I talked to many of them, and some of them were rigid to me and asked me to call them only when I was in Nairobi. They emphasized that it is a waste of time and energy if we do have distance relations.

For a while, I missed Yukari's hug and my friendship with Mia, Sofia, Yukari, and Nur. They were still my most important friends of mine as I had already searched one-third of the globe. For me, the whole searching process was a meaningless addition; my friend's trip to Iran gave meaning to it and my whole life. Finally, I felt it is the moment that I need to talk to Mia immediately. She was the one that I needed to know better to find out why she never felt that bad after our group had separated. I was sure that I needed her mindset more than any other friend. I had to wait for a couple of hours before calling her because of Isfahan and Sydney's time difference. It was around 10:00 A.M when I called her, and she told me that she would call me later as she had already started a hectic day. I had no other options and agreed to wait for her call. I knew that her video call wouldn't be sooner than 5-6 hours, so I started reading a book and pondering the situation I created for myself. While thinking about my view for the future, I noticed that I already knew that I didn't want to be like some heroes in sad books. After all, I have already passed the phase that I used to feel hollow in my life. I noticed what I don't want to be, but if I am not a sad hero, what would I want to be? It was the time that I felt a new energy in myself. I kind of woke up from a deep sleep, and I started making positive pictures for my future. I started planning to buy new stuff for myself and find new real friends in Iran. It is my time and my turn to create a positive wave in my life, not waiting for other people's opinions to like or reject me. I was in that mood that I fell into a deep sleep.

When Mia finally called, I was in such a different mood that she mentioned it immediately; all I wanted was my friends and me together, something that was too silly that I was laughing at it when I told her. Okay, listen to me, Mohammad, she said. You need to redress your thoughts before asking a new person to come into your life. Your thoughts are chaotic right now and nobody, let me emphasize, nobody would accept to be with you because right now, you are a high-risk option for any girl in your life. Whatever is your reason, hugging a girl shouldn't bring any special feelings for someone in your situation. You are not that old to remember things past and get emotional. Don't lose your upward view and enjoy every moment of your life. Even if I am your soulmate, still go and pay for sex for a while and stay away from marriage and your fantasy world.

It was too odd hearing what she said. Her cute voice had something inside that I told myself; her advice comes from her good feelings about me. I said that I was thinking about a funny future, what???? She screamed! I said it would be very funny if we married and we needed a short break in our relations, you will pay for sex during that time for me. We both laughed, and she told me it would never happen in the real world, especially if we married. I shared my thoughts about her initial impact on me and the way that I wanted to forget about my religious beliefs. She was mature enough to understand this joke, and we had great times on the phone with her family members. Her father mentioned that he followed my last online tournament and is proud that he has a friend that is such a strong chess player. He added that I am telling that because of Mia because she likes you and made me say that. Now, it was my turn to understand his father's joke and act like someone that whole the world doesn't belong to him.

CHAPTER FOUR

When I decided to be a better version of myself, I knew that I could not change all aspects of my life dramatically. For my readers that have basic chess knowledge, I should describe my situation as a beginner who tries to win more and more games by changing his openings. We all knew that it works till a certain time when your opponents understand the depth of your thoughts, and then you will be surprised by players with better basic chess knowledge. I noticed my first step should be getting ready for more steps with girls, not only being a shallow guy that avoids physical interactions with girls because of his belief system.

These ideas were with me for the following two weeks, and I was searching about my steps and how I could change. As an active chess champion, I knew that I should change or be changed and replaced by new players, so I asked myself whether I wanted to live my life like what I had to be as a chess player. Do I want to change every time, or can I look at my wife as a safe zone in my life where I can be myself, and I should ask her to accept me as who I am?

A very simple solution for me was forgetting about all my feelings in KL and everyone that I knew and fleeing from the fact that Mia was right.

Nowadays, when a chess player needs to get ready for a stronger opponent, S/he could easily use his/ her computer and find a solution for positions that he has no idea about the story behind them, but in the past, there were times that you had only your books and some friends as your teammates. Again imagine the situation that you are the best player of your generation, and you already had found many mistakes in chess books. In that situation, I remembered Mikhail Botvinnik, one of the most influential players of all time that once lost his title, and he needed to win the last game of the match to remain the world's chess champion in his match versus David Bronstein.

It was exactly my situation. My friends had less information than me about the situation that I stocked in it, and there were no websites on the internet to help me with this situation. It was me and only me.

In chess tournaments, I usually easily accept that my opponent was better than me, and I will try to better off myself in the next tournament. In fact, I use the time factor to solve or wane this problem. For now, I tried to accept the fact that I am not qualified for a serious love till later that could redress my thoughts and mindset about life.

I stayed away from my idea for a while, concentrating on my work, chess tournaments, and piano lessons. I always wanted to learn how to play my favorite songs instead of learning the basics of music, so I searched for a relaxing piece of music. It was the time that I watched a masterpiece by Yiruma called "A river flows in you." That piece of music made me think about life again and again. I was separated from everyone and every old-fashion habit in my life. Why do I need love? I asked myself. Isn't it better to stay single for the rest of my life? I would be able to travel and search many places in the world and keep learning till the last moment of my life.

Staying single for the rest of my life looked like a brilliant idea till one day that I noticed as a Muslim, I was not allowed to do that. This huge duality in my mind had impacted my results in all aspects of my life. It mostly could be seen in the tournaments that I started losing my games versus my previous students. It rang in my head that I was losing my time and energy on things that would not matter a few years later. I stock with Kuala Lumpur, Nairobi, and Novisad for a long time among all cities that I searched and visited. Besides those cities, I had a serious option in Sydney that had to be solved too. I had two choices for the following trips. The first one was solving my emotional issues by visiting Sydney or KL or using the second plan and going forward without looking at the past. An old version of me naturally could prefer the second scenario in which I could restart my relations in a whole different world which was equal to changing my opening in a new chess tournament. My decision to be a better version of myself made me make a plan based on my first option.

Visiting Australia was a time-consuming process as I had to try to get a tourist visa that needed many documents that could turn into a long process. It was the moment that I decided about my future destination, visiting Kuala Lumpur for the second time!

Most people that I knew told me it is not a clever action that you visit a foreign country for the second time while you already like many places that you couldn't visit and have this opportunity to visit them.

When I wanted to tell my friends about my decision for my upcoming holidays, I thought that if Yukari and Mia were analyzing me as a serious option, they would join me in KL. I was sure about Sofia as she was living in the KL. Sooner I understood that we were living in a chaotic world. Nobody plans for his or her life to be matched with you. After calling Yukari, she told me that she had to work too hard because she was near her project's deadline at that time. The fact that we have different holidays than most countries around the world was making me crazy. I was sure that she is telling the truth, and I saw that rejecting my offer couldn't be considered a no to our relationship.

Mia also told me that she prefers to see me in another city than KL because she wants to visit more countries.

Being a new person is not that easy, and I am sure that I am not the type of guy who remembers that they are in such a process or make a to-do list for my routine life. At that moment, I decided to postpone my decision till a better time when I could think more clearly about my future.

Later I noticed that my decision about my trip was a reaction to Mia, and I wanted to prove that nobody could tell me that I was appropriate to do or achieve something in my life.

When you are not ready for a big step like this in your life, but you want just do it, you should accept its consequences. In my case, being tired of people on the one hand and feeling pressure from my religious thoughts, on the other hand, created a situation for me that I had no way to escape from it.

In spite of all challenges in my way, I know something for sure that is I have a dream to meet a girl in another country and experience true love with her. What I want for sure is something that will change the race of my family from a pure middle eastern to a mixture of middle eastern with another place.

In this journey, I plan to make this book an opportunity for all my readers to feel free to ask me to search in their hometown for what a normal human being could call true love.

To my dear readers:

I plan to start my next short story from where we ended now, and I want to ask you to feel free to join this journey with me by your votes, whether to suggest me a new destination or concentrate on one of the characters of this book.

I hope you all see this book as an opportunity to be in an international endeavor to send a message for upcoming generations to make a difference with what they received from what human beings could receive during history. I hope we all send this message that we can always be better by being thankful and creative.

The second book will start after receiving one hundred book reviews.

All of you are very important to me. Let's break some stereotypes for the next generations.

Regards,
Mohammad Soltanian

www.ingramcontent.com/pod-product-compliance
Lightning Source LLC
Chambersburg PA
CBHW051135160726